Margaret Nash

Grace to the
Rescue!

Illustrated by Cheryl Tarbuck

MACDONALD YOUNG BOOKS

540747

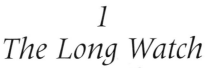

1
The Long Watch

Grace Darling pushed back the bed
blankets and sat up.

Was that Father calling? She couldn't
tell for the pounding of the waves on
the lighthouse wall.

"G-r-a-c-e!" She hurried to the spiral staircase.

Yes, he was a few steps beneath her. His hair looked wild, and his face was white in the lamplight.

"Grace, I fear we must go outside and tie up the coble. The storm is getting worse than ever."

"I'll be right down, Father."

She pulled on a heavy skirt, grabbed her scarf, and hurried down to the kitchen. One mighty wave could wreck their treasured fishing boat. And then what would they do? Father was ready, with a coil of rope in his hands.

"Hold on to me, Grace, it's wild out there."

But the moment he opened the door, the wind separated them and hurled a mountain of spray over her.

"Grace!"

"I'm all right, Father. Get the boat."

He managed to drag it across the rocks, but it took all their strength, with the wind screaming and tearing at their clothes, for them to tie it safely.

They waded back indoors exhausted.

"Thank goodness that's done," he
said, wiping beads of water off his chin.
"This is the worst storm since we moved
here, and that was all of twelve years
ago." Grace handed him a towel.

She remembered moving into the
Longstone lighthouse with its curved
cupboards when she was ten years old.

"I was so excited I gave myself a
headache," she said.

Her father tried to smile but it turned
into a yawn, and Grace thought how
tired he looked.

"Why don't you go to bed, Father
and let me take over the watch? I'll not
sleep now."

"If you're sure, Grace." She nodded.

"Go on, Mother will have made the
bed warm for you. I'll check the lantern
now."

She was proud of their lantern and its help to seamen. She enjoyed cleaning its reflectors and polishing the brasswork around it.

Everything was fine. The burners were all working. There was plenty of oil in the lamps, and there were no distress signals out at sea.

Grace went back to her bedroom and sat beside the window. It was only midnight. She watched the ghostly reflection of the beam pass over the water. It would be a long watch this night, before the pale light of dawn appeared.

2
The Wreck at Dawn

Grace stretched her arms and yawned. The storm was still raging and the clock on the wall showed it to be just after four.

Through the spray splattered window she could just see the rocks starting to push out of the gloom. Little Harcar Rock was always first, with Big Harcar lumped behind it. But Big Harcar looked strange, as though there was a bulge on its side.

Oh no, not a boat. Oh please no!
A wall of sea rose up the rock and the
bulge disappeared. But the waves fell
back in ribbons and it was a boat –
jagged, grim and awful.

"Father, a wreck. Father!" She could hear him flinging himself out of bed and dashing across the floor. She didn't wait.

Up the steepest twist of the spiral she climbed to the lantern platform at the top of the lighthouse. Immediately he was behind her in his bare feet. She passed him the telescope. "Big Harcar, western corner." She saw his face pull into tight lines.

"I'm going out."

"Father, your feet!"

"No matter."

Grace turned and saw her mother coming up the spiral with his boots. She didn't often come so far, for the spiral was narrow, and Mrs. Darling was amply proportioned.

"Mother…!" Grace helped her up the top steps.

Then Father was back in, shaking his head.

"It's a boat all right. It's hung on the rock like a coat on a peg – a dreadful sight, and all we can do is watch and wait for daylight." Grace looked across the stretch of water. The blackness lay like a carpet over the sea. If only they could roll it back and see things clearly.

For three hours they watched and waited, passing the telescope anxiously between the three of them. Then Father saw the roundness of a wheel.

"It's the Forfarshire paddle steamer." He moved the telescope to his other eye. "I can see the mast too."

"Oh Father surely not!" He nodded sadly.

"But there would be lots of people on board."

She took the telescope. It was indeed the luxury paddle steamer, of which everyone was so proud. She scanned across the rocks, a few centimetres at a time, then stopped.

"There are people." Her father reached for the telescope, but she hung on to it. "Survivors, Father. We've got to save them."

"No," said Mrs. Darling. "Not with your brother over at Seahouses. Who would row?"

"I'll row," said Grace.

"Grace, you could both perish." But Grace was already at the spiral and climbing down to prepare for the rescue.

3
The Swollen Sea

She collected blankets from the service room, then took off her long petticoats, for fear they would be a hindrance. She tied a scarf over her head and hurried downstairs. Mrs. Darling was following her husband round the kitchen.

"You can't go, you can't. Not without Brooks. Please William, think no more of it."

"The Seahouses lifeboat will not go in these gales woman, it's up to us. A hot drink would be useful." Her mother ignored him and went on pleading. Grace put on her working coat, and made a can of hot tea. She grabbed her shawl.

"Ready, Father."

"You're sure about going now, Grace?"
She nodded.

Her mother was standing by the door,
her arms out like barriers.

"Oh Grace…"

Mr Darling gently moved his wife
aside, and Mrs. Darling, seeing at last
they meant to go, gave in and followed
them out across the slippy rocks. She
held the boat as steady as she could.

There was no time for goodbye's. The boat spun as Grace stepped in and it was all they could do to stay upright.

"The long way round, Grace, between the Longstone and the Blue Caps."

"Yes, Father."

The boat lunged almost vertical as the sea swelled, then plunged down, and water swilled onto them. If they could only get behind Little Harcar the journey would hold promise. Again and again Grace reached into the seething whiteness with the heavy oar.

Then suddenly Father was shouting "well done" and they were through the stretch known as Crawford's Gut, and in the lee of Little Harcar. "Keep going, Grace."

The black clouds were rolling. The seabirds were swooping. The waves were rising. And the boat was tossed so that even the rocks themselves seemed to move. But all the time they were getting nearer and she could see men reaching out to them.

"Head for beyond the point," ordered her father, and she felt him heave his oar, and the boat nose into a narrow inlet behind the rock. Two strong strokes and Father was bringing in his oar and standing up. A big wave sprang up the rock and in the seconds it took to run back he leapt off the boat and was across.

4
Rescued off the Rock

The boat almost keeled over and would have thrown Grace into the sea had she not pushed the oar hard against the rock. Now she had to keep it from smashing against the rocks. The wind whipped her. The spray blurred her vision. And all the time the seabirds screeched mockingly as the waves exploded against the rocks.

"Grace!" Father was back with two men, one bleeding badly. Together they lay the injured man down the side of the boat and wrapped him up as best they could.

"Nine alive, three dead, Grace." He leapt ashore again.

"Take care, Father."

The boat was easier to balance with the extra weight and she spared the odd glance towards the Harcar. Why was Father climbing further on the rock with a babe in his arms?

A strip of wood blew on board hitting her legs and distracting her. Debris from the Forfarshire, no doubt! Now there was a bale of cloth buffeting towards them. She pushed it away.

Her arms ached. Her energy was almost spent. Pray one of the men would help row back.

"Grace!" Father was at the water's edge with two more men, and a woman who kept sinking to the ground and wailing.

"Her two babes are dead," he explained. "She's distraught." As the men struggled aboard with the woman the boat listed.

"Quick!" yelled Grace for an oar was sliding into the water. One of the men grabbed it and started pulling against the waves to straighten the boat.

"We've got to go, Father," said Grace.
She rowed with the man, who though
cut and shaken rowed well, and by the
time Father joined them they were out
of the inlet, and on their way back to
the lighthouse. It was easier with three
rowing but as they turned into
Crawfords Gut the wind hit them full
blast and they had to battle against it.

"Give us strength, Miss!" pleaded the
man and Grace could see he was tiring.

"We're nearly home, Sir," said Grace, "only a few more minutes."

It had been her silent prayer too, that strength would be given them. But it had been, for the rocks of the Longstone were coming nearer and nearer and she could see a figure standing there. A sudden wash of the waves brought them right alongside the Longstone and there was Mother, tears in her eyes, reaching out to help.

5
Safe in the parlour

The wind was still howling round the
lighthouse and the waves lashing the
walls. Grace rested her aching back
against the door and looked round the
steamy parlour. It was full of tired
bodies, crowded like peas in pods,
beneath the drying clothes. Father and
another had fetched the four remaining
survivors, and her brother Brooks had
arrived with six members of the
Seahouses lifeboat crew who had gone
to the wreck later and were unable to
get back for the storm.

"It were a nightmare. It were a nightmare!" The man huddled in the corner by the fire kept on and on repeating these words.

"You're safe now," said Grace. "We're all safe."

She'd cooked every vegetable in the house for them, and dished out all the rabbit broth. Mother had bandaged their wounds, and Father, in an attempt to comfort everyone, had handed round his precious drinking bottle. Now at last it was more peaceful in the parlour.

Grace left them, and slowly dragged herself up to her room.

The beam of the lantern swung across the rolling sea. She saw it pass over the Harcar rocks. It seemed days, not hours, since she'd first spotted the wreck.

She didn't hear Father and Mother
come into the room for her thoughts
were still on the rescue. Thank goodness
they'd made it. Father came beside her
and stood watching the beam too.

"Well, Grace, we did what we could.
Proud I am, to have a courageous
daughter like you."

"You were right to go lass," said
Mother. "Those people will be grateful to
you for the rest of their lives."

And they were. Everyone was, for
Grace received many many gifts and
there came an endless stream of visitors
to the lighthouse.

"I wish things would calm down, Mother," said Grace, looking out of her window months later, "like the sea does!" The waves were barely nibbling the base of the Harcar at that moment.

"You'll have some peace today though," said Mrs. Darling. Grace smiled. She certainly would, for she was crossing to the mainland to look for spring flowers, a rare treat.

"Why don't you wear your new dress and gold locket, Grace?"

The gold locket was her most treasured gift, and it was all the thanks she'd ever really wanted. It was from the survivors. Inside it, on a green velvet base, lay nine hairs entwined in a circle – one from the head of each of them.

Grace let the locket dangle in the sunlight a moment before fastening it round her neck and patting it lovingly.

Then holding her skirts, she went downstairs and out across the rocks towards the sea which was calm and blue and still as a mill pond. You could see for miles. There'd be no wrecks today.